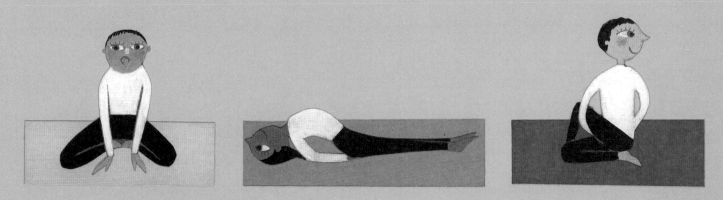

My Daddy is a Pretzel

Yoga for Parents and Kids

"I am a teacher. A teacher is someone who leads.
There is no magic here. I do not walk on water.
I do not part the sea. I just love children"
— *Marva Collins*

Introduction

When I was a boy, the adults in my life helped me to find figures who possessed qualities worth striving for: athletes and explorers with exceptional powers of perseverance and self discipline; martial artists who had mastered both body and mind; politicians and other agents of social change who dared to face the unknown, standing up for what deserved to be loved and protected; and spiritual leaders who possessed the traits of character we most admire: honesty, compassion and courage. As I grew older, I learned that noble people (heroes) could be found closer to home too – among my neighbors, friends, and family members … in fact my own parents were courageous pioneers in helping to establish yoga in America.

Looking back, I see how lucky I was that my parents and so many of my teachers thought it was worthwhile to practice yoga, to meditate and to pay attention to their physical and spiritual health. Their commitment gave me a "picture" of what vitality and virtue looked like and showed me how I could apply these ideals to my own life. Now, as a parent in turn, I set out to share these same ideals with my three sons, practicing yoga with them and encouraging them to do their best and achieve their potential. With this book, I hope to help you too. The practices here give children and adults alike targets to aim for and examples to follow, while the storyline shows how the benefits and inner meanings of the yoga postures relate to the way we live, whatever our profession or status in life.

As every parent understands, children imitate what they see, hear and feel. They naturally look for examples to follow. Although

children have an inner compass that points them toward a true north, they do not know the difference between habits that give life and habits that take life away. They simply imitate and do what they see, hear and experience. So it makes a big difference when we adults make efforts to give direction and show what habits lead to a vital, healthy and happy life.

In this book, I set out to share with you the time-honored task of training the hearts, minds and bodies of the young. This task involves explicit training in good habits, and it involves the example of adults who, through their daily behavior, show children that they take spiritual virtue and physical vitality seriously — but not without losing their sense of humor! The message and the practices in these pages will help children to enjoy the benefits and rewards of yoga practice. It is never too early to start. These postures and the philosophy behind them have the power to impress themselves upon young minds and to remain as lifelong guides, as tools for practice and signposts that point the way.

My goal is to present health and virtue not as something to possess or to *have*, but as something to *be* — as the most important thing to be. As we read this story to our children and practice the postures, we begin to acquaint them with the idea that the life of good health, and the life of virtue and vitality, is worth living. We invite them to lift their young eyes, to reach up and to grow into brave and powerful young people. For it is by striving for the best in ourselves that we empower our children and show them that they too can live with the nobility of heroes.

BARON BAPTISTE

Today, in class, we're going to say
What jobs our parents do each day.

Niki says her mommy's a gardener.

Sometimes, my daddy's a tree.

The Tree Pose
Vrksasana

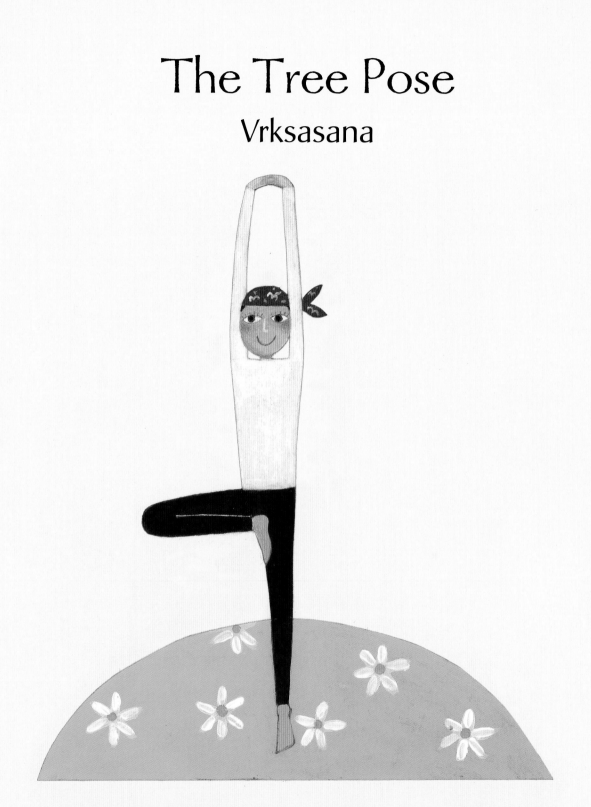

The tree pose teaches us to support ourselves with strong roots, so that we can reach high and remain stable, yet be flexible, at the same time.

1 Stand straight with your feet below your hips.

2 Inhale and lift your right foot up to your inner thigh.

3 Bring your hands together at your heart center.

4 Sweep your arms up above your head.

5 Interlace your fingers, palms up, and stretch tall.

6 When you are ready, lower your arms and your right foot as you exhale.

Lionel says his parents are vets.

Sometimes, my daddy's a dog.

The Dog Pose
Adho Mukha Svanasana

Have you noticed how supple dogs are when they stretch? The dog pose teaches us to be humble and accept our bodies as they are, because almost anyone can practice it, and as with anything, practice makes progress.

1 Kneel on your bottom with your head on the floor and your arms stretched out in front of you.

2 Push back on your heels and raise your bottom so that you make a triangle.

3 Push down into your heels toward the floor and make sure your spine is straight.

4 Hold the pose for as long as you can, then lower your bottom back onto your heels, and rest for a while with your head on the floor before you sit up.

If you can't straighten your back, it is a good idea to practice this pose with your knees bent.

Chang says his mom's an architect.

Sometimes, my daddy's a triangle.

The Triangle Pose
Trikonasana

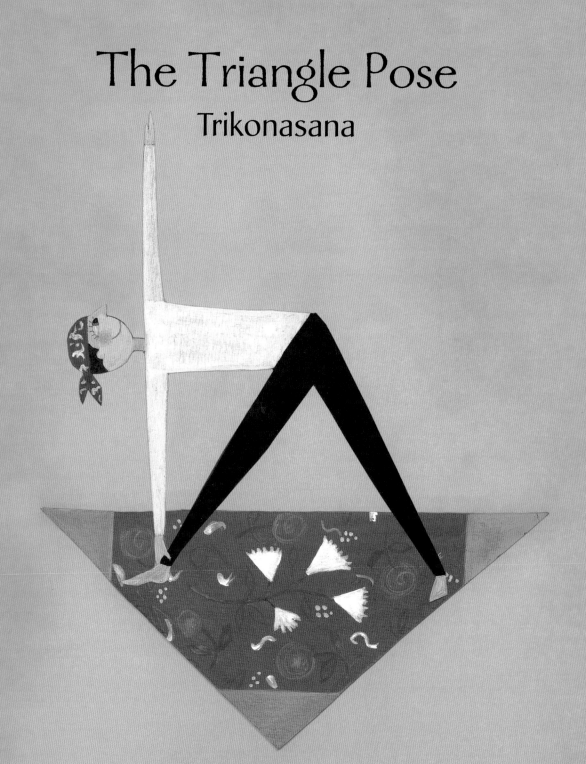

Triangles are the most stable of the geometric shapes. The triangle pose teaches us to be strong, to build a foundation of support and to relax under pressure. Triangles have three sides and three angles – just as we have three aspects: mind, body and spirit.

1 Jump your feet apart and stretch out your arms at the same time.

2 Turn your right foot so that its heel points to the center of your left foot.

3 As you exhale, tilt your upper body from the waist over to the right until your right hand reaches your right ankle. Inhale.

4 Now exhale and turn your head to look up at your left thumb.

5 To come out of the pose, reverse these movements.

6 Repeat on the left side.

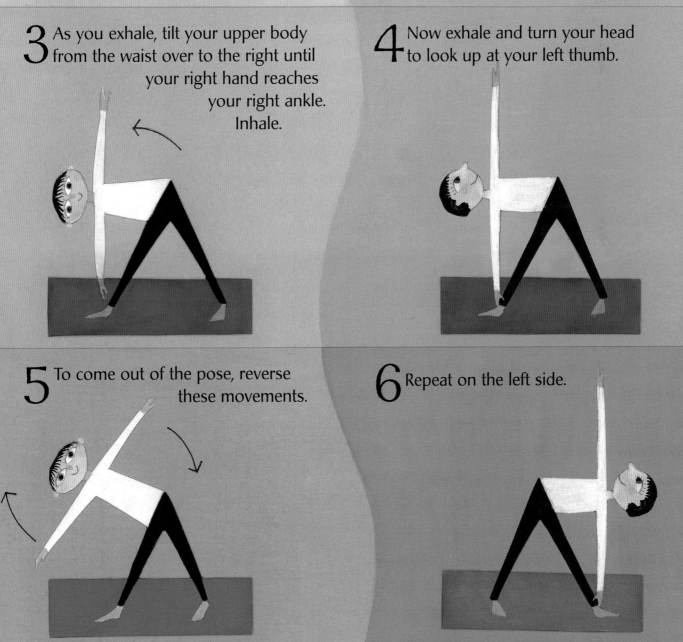

Anna says her step-dad's a pilot.

Sometimes, my daddy's an airplane.

The Airplane Pose
Dekasana

Like an airplane that flies high in the sky, this pose teaches us
to believe in ourselves so that we can soar through life.
Practice this posture on both sides and don't worry if you
wobble!

1 Stand up straight and raise your right leg so that your thigh is parallel to the floor.

2 Place your hands on your hips and bring your right knee in to your chest.

3 As you exhale, stretch your right leg straight out behind you and swing your upper body forward, until you are parallel to the floor.

4 Stretch out your arms behind you like wings, palms down.

Malachi says his daddy's a builder.

Sometimes, my daddy's a bridge.

The Bridge Pose
Setu Bandhasana

Ride the changes! Like a bridge that joins one place to another, this pose teaches us to remain strong as we move from one life stage to the next, but also to be flexible, so that we don't break when the winds of change are fierce.

1 Lie on your back with your feet hip-width apart.

2 Slide your heels beneath your knees. As you inhale, tilt your pelvis and lift up your hips until you are on your shoulders.

3 Pull your shoulder blades inward and bring your hands together under your back, arms straight

4 Hold the pose for as long as you are comfortable, then lower your body carefully to the floor.

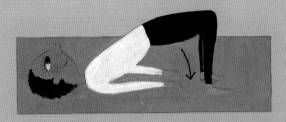

Emmie says her daddy's a farmer.

Sometimes, my daddy's a plow.

The Plow Pose
Halasana

Like the plow that turns the soil over to make way for new growth, this pose teaches us that overturning old ways of seeing things sets the ground for inner growth. If we plow well, we can sow well, and then reap the rewards of what we have planted.

1 Lie on your back and bring your knees into your chest.

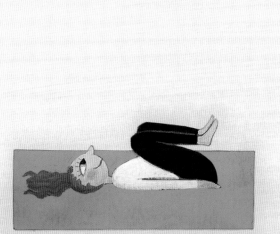

2 As you exhale, raise your legs and hips straight up, rolling onto the back of your shoulders and using your hands to support your back. Inhale.

3 As you exhale, lower your legs behind your head toward the floor.

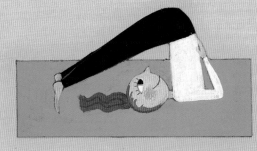

4 To come out of the pose, reverse these movements.

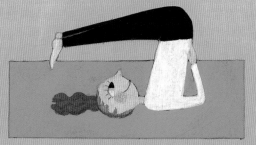

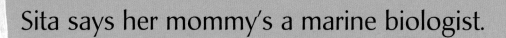 Sita says her mommy's a marine biologist.

Sometimes, my daddy's a fish.

The Fish Pose
Matsyasana

The fish pose teaches us how to relax and accept the flow
of life that carries and supports us on our journey – don't
struggle upstream, jump in and just go with the flow, even in
turbulent times.

1 Sit on the floor with your legs straight and your hands under your bottom, palms down, toes pointed.

2 Lean back until your forearms are on the floor. Pull your elbows, forearms and shoulder blades close together.

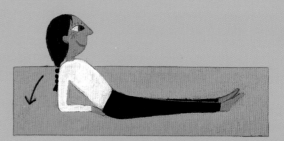

3 As you inhale, arch your back, lower your head and slide back until your crown is resting on the floor.

4 To release the pose, bring your arms back to your sides and slowly uncurve until you are lying flat on the floor.

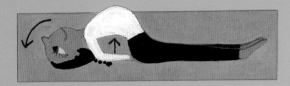

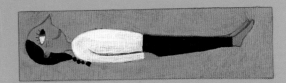

Pedro says his daddy works in Africa.

Sometimes, my daddy's a lion.

The Lion Pose
Simhasana

Lions are brave and they have fierce roars! This pose
encourages us to feel and express our power and courage.
It challenges us to be bold, and to overcome our fears.

1 Kneel on the floor with your bottom on your heels.

2 Separate your legs at the knees.

3 Lean forward and place your hands in front of you, fingers pointing out.

4 Tuck in your chin, stick your tongue out and roar!

I say my mommy's a baker,

And sometimes my daddy's a pretzel!

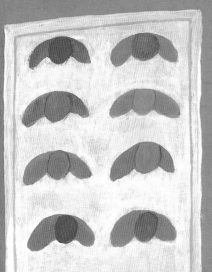

The Pretzel Pose (Seated Twist)
Marichyasana

The spine is the center of the body and the center of the
nervous system. Practicing the seated twist helps us to release
all kinds of tensions. And just as the body benefits, so too
does the mind, letting go of unnecessary thoughts and
worries, and becoming confident, open and alert.

1 Bend your right knee and slide your right leg under your left leg, tucking your right foot against your left hip.

2 Draw up your left leg and lift your left foot over your right knee, with the toes pointing forward.

3 Exhaling, twist to the left, starting at the base of the spine, and placing your left hand about a foot behind you for support.

4 Slide your right arm under your left thigh or, if you cannot manage this, press your right elbow against your left knee to give you more leverage.

5 Link your hands together behind your back and twist as far as possible to the left, turning your head to look behind you.

6 Repeat the movement on the other side, following the same sequence.

YOGA IS POWER!

Tree

Dog

Triangle

Airplane

Yoga and Your Life

✦ Yoga is more than a way of exercising; it's also a way of life. Don't just do the postures; think about what they mean to you and relate them to what's happening in your world.

✦ Yoga can help you get unstuck if you are unhappy about something in your life. Explore the postures and focus on the ones that are most important to you. For example, if there is a lot of change happening in your life, you can build yourself a bridge — in fact, you can be your own bridge. If you are feeling afraid or nervous, you can boost your courage with the lion pose.

✦ The physical demands of yoga teach you how to navigate and negotiate many challenges. Achieving physical strength, alignment, balance, flexibility and integration takes focus, determination and finesse. You can apply these skills to other areas of your life.

✦ If you practice with your mom or your dad, or your schoolteacher, don't fool around but don't be too serious either. Do what you can and have fun.

✦ Bring your yoga skills to the other areas of your life. For instance, at school use your yoga skills of relaxing, focusing and concentrating during a difficult test, or practice using more patience, respect and confidence with your friends.

✦ This book is just one step on your yoga journey. If you enjoy it, and you want to know more, find out if there are any yoga classes in your neighborhood or ask your schoolteacher to set up a class. It's fun to practice yoga in a group, and you can learn fast if you have a good teacher — just like the children in this story!

Barefoot Books
Celebrating Art and Story

At Barefoot Books, we celebrate art and story with books that open
the hearts and minds of children from all walks of life, inspiring them to read
deeper, search further, and explore their own creative gifts. Taking our
inspiration from many different cultures, we focus on themes that encourage
independence of spirit, enthusiasm for learning, and acceptance of other
traditions. Thoughtfully prepared by writers, artists and storytellers from
all over the world, our products combine the best of the present with the best
of the past to educate our children as the caretakers of tomorrow.

www.barefootbooks.com

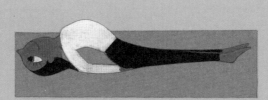